The Old Lacquered Box

Milicent G. Tycko

authorHOUSE®

AuthorHouse™
1663 Liberty Drive
Bloomington, IN 47403
www.authorhouse.com
Phone: 1 (800) 839-8640

Published by AuthorHouse 02/23/2018

ISBN: 978-1-5462-3080-9 (sc)
ISBN: 978-1-5462-3079-3 (e)

Library of Congress Control Number: 2018902429

Print information available on the last page.

Contents

The Old Lacquered Box

In an old lacquered box, about 12 by 10 by 8 inches, there quietly sat little notebooks holding some previously typed writing and also many original penciled writing with cross-outs and additions on a motley mix of papers. The order in which all this paper emerged, once the lid of the box was lifted, was only roughly inverse to the chronological order in which they were written suggesting that a few desultory attempts to organize the writings were superceeded by the spontaneous thrusting of additional papers into the old lacquered box from time to time.

Now is the moment of truth, when the contents of the box ask to be arranged neatly. Now is the time to type away indiscriminantly without editing or remorse or introspection—it is just the way it is. Perhaps when Winter comes and life becomes more snow-bound, it will give time to muse about the events, moods, stages of existence which surrounded these writings. If Winter becomes snow-bound and interminable, then this project of preserving and loosely ordering the aforementioned papers might be fulfilled.

So the ensuing 54 pages embrace a good deal of the papers stashed in the old lacquered box, with some numbers and dates available.

written over many years by Milicent G. Tycko
2007

My Words

True to my love of you, my words,
I strengthen my love in the midst
Of sorrowful times when miasmas
Of killing and maiming and hate reports
Persist in their thickening presence.

A year marked by loss is this 2001
And a threat of more to come
So my love of you, words,
Is a salve to my hurt
And will strengthen my love of all else.

My grandchildren must have a life of
Joy and share in clear air with all
Children who dance on this globe.

For those much like seedlings which
Sprout all about, these words may be water
That nourishes all, for these words are the
Shadows of thought and of mood
Yearning and reaching for all that is good.

Actions can form the historic events
While words emanate from the pitiful
Souls of us humans who strive to
Endure through the years

And most certainly will
When our words sing along to
Describe and emote and be treasured
As beautiful shells from the sea.

August 2002

I love my flowers

Trio

Viola

It is bleak in the forest that I go through. The trees appear to be hung like black cardboard lanterns in oily and licorice profusion. There is no acquittal from this somber, cavernous wood. Brambled pathways wind about the trees as rasping viola phrases straining to sing in shadowy muted and nightmare-blunted cries. It is forever pre-dawn. The forest scurryings have lost their urgent edge and rustle, blunted now into a hushed and mournful wait. Darkness is prolonged. The prose of nature halted.

Cello

A young lady in her mercerized cotton plaid exploded brightly into the streets, never being sad. She had a good time night and a razzle flashing grin, and it was welcome, welcome hallelujah world. Like a shiny glowing cello with its curves intact, she opened up a furrow through the turbid air. Oval and glorious, supple and sane, her sonorous way was knuckled along in grace.

Violin

A consumer par excellence, briefcase in hand, wended his way at noon over regular slates that glistened like windwashed, watery stones. Regularized, geometrized and paced accordingly, he let himself reflect the building grids of windows and walls, as an inverse waffle. His rightangled way into restaurant and shops was eased by doormen near doorsteps. Glancing on displays, as a violin in clarity, his walk flowed on. It figured prominently in no headlines, yet in innocence and speed, it sang out surely and was comfortable, confined in range.

Glissando round a corner, embraced by outside chaos, the line of march was stranger to all doubt. Sidewalks paced in intervals for hard-cash purchase purposes, formed taut-stringed streets to play upon. His violin city.

The trio ended. We applauded and we left the concert hall, after hearing Mozart's Divertimento.

1977 #1

Summer Wanderings

A cow is lazy and incumbent
Not insolvent though
Having its milk assets

But incumbent as it
Stands upon its grass
Slope displaying

Mass in white and black

Regally possessing space in shape of cow
Unseatable and stolid now.

A furzed farm under rainbow glass water drop
Enlarging wheat
Enlarging bugs
Enlarging spiked and sticky stalks
Clear beauty under rainbow glass
Velvet growth of pulsing farm

Cornea captured
Sweetened by bees

Colored by birds
Made gaudy by eggplants and berries and grapes
Seen large under glass
As the blood in the seed of the pomegranate fruit
Is shielded and sought through
Translucent hard walls.

1978 #2

On A Visit to the Guggenheim Museum

Reframed

Pried from the lid of Rembrandt's coffin
All reliquary status
Removed   regained   renewed
From shadowy tomb

Placed against a concrete wall
Vast dazzling museum white
For a rough and frozen frame
The lone board floats

Proclaimed   produced   purified
Silent hard streak of black
A long songless stroke
At last attaining
Pure line

Arrived and baptized
minimal art
min. art

Nothing is lost
Nothing is lost
Ever ever

1980 #3

Tawny

Yes my dear darkling
My soul all numb and grey
Longs towards your
Fine and tawny
Forehead shining

Solid and molded
Of flaming tender iron
No form exists of all
The vapid brushstrokes
Which people the air
But that one solid
Tawny head of yours
I draw it from the
Gauzy unreal world
Directly to me

Solid it sits
Upon my breast
Where our breaths combine
I am dizzy from the
Wonder of it all.

1983 #4

Blue Slates

The image I had
of damp blue slates
Scattered in grass with pine sprigs upon them
Waited for days to find privacy
And become spoken.

Meanwhile so many other distractions
Whirled in a blur
It seemed hopeless to grasp that first
Sensation which cried as trampled upon.

Weary and happy thoughts and events
Layered themselves as stifling insulation
And oppressed my dream.

Yet with piercing keeness the slates surfaced
Again and tempted me to concentrate
Upon their damp blue stone.

In my mind I imagined that
My bare feet touched the damp
And dared to feel the tender points of pine
And, lord forgive, by doing so
Were not eternally alone.

1983 #8

February Self

Sometimes I float obliquely through the fog
But otherwise
I try for logarithmic sails
Above the snow-patched fields
And other farm-like
Attributes of earth
Mainly to avail myself
Of sadness in its liquid state

Then within
There lies a sodden doom
A mood of undislodgeable and moor-like mass

The lost the unforgiven

Small raindrops tinkling on the glass of my soul
Provide a melody of counteracting song
In which I seek delight and find
Liquid lyrics which succeed in
Separating me from self

A semi-detached mind gazes on curtains blown
Merely gauze billowing between earth and self
As bandages laid carressingly on wounds
Assuaging fitful pain as parts approach

Obedient and melancholy all the earth lies fitfully
Beneath the snow
And tries to sing itself to sleep
Without a message or a note

Infrequently yet blessedly
The slanted rain draws sadness out
Enabling mood to crystallize upon each drop
Alleviating gloom

Cut not hurt not cry not wail not write not
Weep not be not lose not sing not
So states the rain so states the snow so states the fog
So states the wound so states the sound
Released in song the noteless voice
Permits itself yet cannot

Obedient and melancholy all the earth lies fitfully
Beneath the snow and tries to sing itself to sleep.

1983 #5

Ladies

Wombless we avoid the tomb
And hope for sunny days
Laid out in ardent green

Ladies whose sap has flowed
To fill the veins and souls
Of sons loved dearly

We walk about with aging flesh
That grasps the ovoid hollow
Ladies looking back
With sighs

Who among us mourns
With no relief however?

Montauk Stay

I fear to leave the somber salty sea
Which pulls me back incessantly
In thrallful threnody

A pile of poems is sharply ground
By endless grains of sand
The selfsame grains which kept your tread
From raucous roaring waves

The chorus grows in rushing green
Awash with foam
I fear to leave the somber salty sea
Which holds your tread eternally.

1984 #10

February Elegy

For this very February bemoaned and
Restless in leafy edged sadness
For the decade of pond wooded snows
Window gazed in thought

For this very February as summer and
Continuing wintry spring out of season now

With aged grasshoppers stretching in their
Useless strivings over
Long lying brown and wet logs lain in fixed
Patterns caught in leafy snow by etching light
A steadiness does prevail though caught in
Leaf quivering anguish watching
Grasshoppers too enfeebled to do their work

Desolate logs long lain in silent woods
During February summers and summer itself
As drawn in chalky waves of grey

The snowy woods remain cross-hatched
With fallen trees   The breath of
little ones no longer
Adds to mist of pond and leaf decay

It seems the trees are ultimate groom and ultimate bride

Through whose fingers ran the breath of child
Through whose fingers brushed the sigh of age
Through whose long lost lying logs
The sad crisp leaves were shed as tears of
Fungal white in still futility.

1983 #6

Kitchen Thoughts

Everything seems vague
Out of touch
And ill-fitting

Even the old cat's meow
Sounds strong and urgent
Piercing my failing nerves

Wrong for putting
Into ordered song
A day of dampness filming
Over Spring surges
Buds thickening with syrup
Awash in rain

I can't give battle
Here's your fish.

1985 #11

Lilacs

Unbelievable
That in the midst of dry brown pine needles
And ice-etched frost pools of fallen leaves
There dares to stand now
A new crocus blown to full purple

Which leads the doubter further
Towards the worn out tangle of
Wildrose branches
Hanging sullen after
Winter's wild beating

In which a wooden tub was placed
Containing last year's lilac plant
A brittle barren stand of sticks
Near to spruce and hidden by pine
Supported by a mound of snow
For shelter's sake

Unbelievable
That now

When finger cracks through crusty film
Of frost to find
Stored cold water
And all the yard is mud

The wooden tub of sticks
Proclaims
I am and will be more
For see the pulpy buds I raised

While you bemoaned the winter's wild

Soon these juicy tips will burst
And lilacs, lilacs, lilacs shout

And that's what Nature's all about.

1985 #12

Florida

Inland on grassy seas
Brahmin bulls roam aimlessly
Their molasses earth is thickly bound
With fields of matted stems
Danced upon by gleaming legs
Of egrets
Locked in partnership
They pluck the flies from
Waiting cows in desultory motion
Adding grace and beauty to the scene
For passersby
Who speed in heat-seared autos

Under thickening skies
Searching for the next motel
The next room chilled and
Facing out upon a pool
While all the dumb and roaming
Beasts continue their ordained parade
In slow and innocent charade.

1985 #15

Final Winter

We do certain things together
Which are physical
Preventing lonely green spaces
Between us
From tinting out to white snow

In mutual consent we do agree
To seek the shelter of our long love
In beneficial harmony

Avoiding imminent desolation of
Brittle limbs forsaken as the branches
Under timeless snow

The sparks fly and you and I
Are pulsing warm and human

Why this avalanche of tears today
Of face contorted to etched grief?

I tremble and shake with sobs
Knowing a final winter comes
And I may someday be alone

A shriveled hapless apple tree
Upon a lonesome hill
Or worse, my love, that you must lie
A cold and lonesome rock without
My arms to cover thee
Or murmur comfort still.

1985 #13

Anniversary Bowl

Clean crystal sits quiet and glowing
(Its nose needs no blowing)
Once washed it retains its lucid depths
Needing less baths than little boys
Whose running and digging
And incessant whirls leave dust

Crystal is full of no surprises
Remaining the same once placed
Upon the table or shelf

It is always there
Reliably catching light and making
Songs of shifting color upon the wall
Each afternoon as the sun lowers

Not as boys who change and grow
And come and go taking your heart
With them

Yet this silent crystal friend
Matters less than the sand it comes from
If breaking it could recreate
The happy laugh or disordered whirl
Of a growing child, a boy.

1985 #14

Tree Dance

Totally black now
Leafless trees of December
Sway stiffly as if
Scratching with dry bristles
On the silver sky

The rushing roar of wind
Drives the brittle dance
Of clumsy trees whose rooted legs refuse to move
While torso arms and hair
Grotesquely wave

An ink-stained cloud
Slides behind the trees
And quickly spreads
To hugely cover

All the silvered set

The trees are robbed of shape
As blackened sky engulfs them
Changing all the set to night.

1985 #16

Frog Poem

The little frog pulsing and moist
It looked at me as I held it in my palm
Then leapt away, I loved it so

Later I held a pink carnellian frog
Carved glossy and cold upon my palm
It sat in weighty silence, I admired it so

Since our breath-ringed love
Must fade awash in tears someday
I write this poem
To freeze our moments still, I wish it so.

1986 #22

Another Spring

I saw the sun twice torn
Hanging low in a luminous sky
The black-fingered trees
Stretched tall and harbored
Chattering clacking volatile birds
Seen to fly in long lean lines

Between the tops of trees
Some heard to whirr above my head
Quicker than that sun changed to a
White jewel or a color-fringed teardrop

The air was frosty
Though Spring insisted
And my delight in nature's joys
This year seemed bittersweet

Oh, oh, I must cry for thinking of
The melted snows and barren dark

Was all the work of Winter
And its stark design which held
Me so securely for so long
To be forgot without a sigh
When prettiness appears in green?

My heart retains its loyalty
To all that's gone
And feels alone as that sole robin
Sitting in the hair of the apple tree
While all the swooping birds form
Webs of song about my head

The shreds of sun fade from the forest screen
I must gather up my limbs from chill

Enough of Spring for now
I'll go indoors and wait.

1986 #19

21

Leaf of Tin (An Elegy)

I want to be a shreeve leaf of tin
For cutting through the crusted earth

Beneath the stone it sharply
Strikes thick iris roots
In web-lanes and
If required it could remove
The teardrop's surface deftly

But in preference remains a tool
For chipping, cutting, digging

People disturbed my routine of
Silence dreams and words

Once when little I spent a day inside my room
Describing shells strung on a copper wire
Brown and white and pink to make a bracelet

It was a gift from my aunt
She's dead now years ago
From cancer filling up her abdomen
Anesthetized by pain she floated to
A white away

The bracelet is also lost
As are my years

I remember writing little girl's words
About those shells so delicate

This memory lies on wet-packed sand
Like the wavy rim of froth left
Upon the beach by waves receding
In salty obscurity

Tides vanish
Nor the tears of salt
Nor the cup of sea
Are useful now
To water iris-roots.

1986 #20

Shore Willow

The much-sketched owl sits plumply on
His roughened bough affirming with alacrity
His wonder and bewilderment
The space abounds with busy flocks
Of birds who whirl about in puzzlement
Flashing as they dart the
Yellow-bright of underwing
Or in a duller raiment singing wondrous songs

In stasis the scene seems embroidered
With thin blue-bodied dragon-flies
Weaving in their flight a knotted path
Of shadowy blue amongst the lilac leaves of
Placid green that hang in simple shapes
Beneath the waving willow stems
That we two also lie beneath thankful for our
Canopied protection as we take delight
In dancing movements of the pale green leaves

And willow stems that shield us so that
We may lie upon this grass together
And forever in a timeless Breughel scene

All geese flow together in their radiance
Of pattern as if seeking anonymity
And gaining it by fleeing cold
In noisy traveling
Skyfuls of geese, but we are
Ignorant of how to flee
For love does bind us in our
Oneness underneath the willow tree
And all we ever need or wanted
Ends in our arbored embrace.

1986 #21

Moth Poem

Exist I brown in abstract gloom
A moth wing dusty and detached
Adheres to my shoe
As I lift it lightly
If only to examine
Striations of archaeological tan
Admixtured with bands of dark brown.

1986 #23

Suburbanites

These are the compromisers plowing along
In their cars lined up for eighty more miles
Along the commuter's straight road
Exhausted each by hours unreckoned
Behind their spoked wheels
They plod as rasping beetles
Creeping ceaselessly
From home to work and back

Clean-shaven and bullied by trucks
They bleed fuel along their line of march
These earnest compromisers
Riveted to jobs within the
City's noisy sphere
They enter their races daily
In the densely crowded rink
Is it bus-shrieks or
Jack-hammers they hear?

Returning then at dusk more limp
Than soldiers used in battle
They sight at last the green lawns
With foliage overcast in peace
And sleep with fixed smiles
Lulled by gurgling cries of owls.

1986 #25

Separate Ponds

We were children together
Beneath the brown bough
Though now we grow wrinkled
As the bark of the oak

Like leaves blown apart
From our sophomoric nest
Gently scattered long ago to
Float on separate ponds.

1987 #24

The Octopus in October

In October an Octopus deftly
Sidled along the
Silky bottom of the large
And sumptuous sea

Forlorn as only he could

Princess
Border Collie

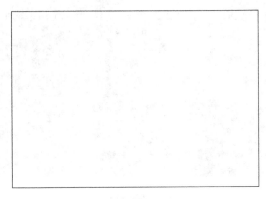

Tippy
Basset Hound

Dog Tippy
Dog Princess

Dog Princess with grandchildren

Dog Princess

Sense the emptiness of the
Sea filled with glowing forms
Of fish and weed yet
Powerless in spite of
Its immensity

To bring its Octopi
The brilliant colors violet
And red and vivid yellow on
Gauguin painted leaves
Those colors dazzling in a
Shameless way the ones who
Emigrated to museums recently
From the sea

So being declared an animal
Of wit and thoughtful mind
In October an Octopus despairingly
Felt like crying for its kind
Doomed to living in dark sea-caves
Though artistically inclined.

1986 #25A

Planetary

Our love is a planet
Which leads us in calculated arcs
Near starry sequels as all the
Heavens surrounding whirl

Long ago a whisper of love
Established the set core of heat

No matter what layers of crystalized ice do
Intervene often in shells of vast time
The spin was determined and veers not awry
Forever returning and circling anew
In love's parabolic design.

Turn of Seasons

Shadowy wooded depths
Glimmer viscously
Seeming to support the Spring-green
Lacquer of newly brushed on buds
Whose tender yellow-green creates
Sufficing grace notes to distract
From deeper forest gloom

Brown-tinged woods abide then
In patient surety
Awaiting turn of seasons
For the spotted leaves to

Crisply fly about in Autumn frost
Settling into forest arms
Which ultimately gather
All leaves
With creaking sighs
To steep and brew in pools of
Still rain on cold earth

Where mushrooms dance in plaintive lines
Ignored in ageless gloom.

1988 #33

Damp Days

Disappointing miasma of
Damp days in May
Heavy with longing and
Soggy with blades of
Cut grass clung to my shoes
A thin trail of green lies
Along the dark hall
As memories dishevelled
And spaced out forlornly
Far from the Spring of
Original growth and joy

The open window lets in
A raucous drill of some
Complaining bird in the woods
Better that the window be
Secured upon a lonely quiet
I hesitate from weakness though
To slam it shut
And brooding at my desk
Am suddenly surprised
To hear a sweet and lilting trill
Of one pulsating bird
Whose song now heard
Relieves my tired soul.

1988 #34

The flakes of snow
Stream down woefully obliging
Gravity and fall over lost
Reservoirs of love forming shadowy
Oases of snow-dunes

When the waters of my sorrow meet
This cold indifferent wall
There is no other way
My arctic tears are whipped to whitest snow
That drifts and blows about the countryside

The winter snows remind me now
Of poetry, of poems transformed

From feelings, sorrows, losses
They sweep across and mass as one
The snowflakes and the sorrow
The shadows and the cold
The fresh and gleaming dune of white
As wondrous as a poem.

1988 #38

Bergen

The clear new sun-stabs
Echo through the craggy

Ancient mountains
Around Bergen, Bergen which
Sits as an old woman by the sea
Holding her wooden houses
In her Hanseatic arms
While her weary legs dangle
In cod-ridden waters
With fish-stalls and flower-carts
Set upon her knees
Bergen you are Bryggen of
King Haakon's huge-halled days
The dark descends from mountains and
Slaps you on the back
But you sing aloud and fiddle
All the more to the sea
And catch your fish and look to mournful
Cliffs cheerfully.

1989 #41

What If I Fall

Who will take care of me?
What if I fall down
While carrying in my arms
A wounded bird to water?
When will I be as a tree
Whose branches laden
With nests of bees and birds
With vines bearing
Exotic flowers that
Glisten sweetly
Shall finally become

So brittle and weak
So aching and tired
That one new petal
Or the few new twigs
Brought to pad a nest
Will snap and bring to earth
This towering burden
Of chirping, buzzing,
Needful life?

I tell myself
In smokey swamps stand

Hardened husks of ancient trees
Whose structure stubbornly persists

Petrified I hope for grace
That I can stand as
A rock, a shell, a frozen shape
In any silhouette
A song, a breath,
An abstract urge
That I can hold up longer
The little nests for creatures
The vines that bear
The glistening berries
The home of bees.

1989 #39

Six Weeks Later

I cannot help it
Much as I try
To look elsewhere upon
The spent cosmos flowers and more
Glowing crimson of zinnias on
Powdery grey of the garden's
Dusty miller plants busy
Embracing and framing the
Violet chrysanthemum buds which
Adore to fly open to sun

No matter I drive to the
Mountain-ringed lakes
And can gaze on dawn's mist
Lying low and ethereal between
The green hills and above
The clear lake there

No matter I walk through museums
And see once again the colors
And lines of the pictures I love
While I wait for slow time to
Push days away

I no longer wake to find myself
Crying in those wrenching sobs
The dreams are now gone
The dreams as if walking through
Series of caves stoney and dark
Then a huge open place ahead with its

Glorious citadel ancient and gleaming
Turrets and domes and high sandy walls
Now it is quiet again
My body no longer a victim of grief

Yet I still cannot help it
The graveside image persists
As I saw them carry a box from some cars

Towards the fresh opened earth in front of me
I realized it really was

My father

And then a giant heavy log
Smote me painfully
Across my face.

1989 #40

Linen Fragments

More intricate my love I cannot be
Embroidering my wishes on a sorrow tree
Of time spent otherwise in empty ways
Sewn images in floss old memories in haze
Preserved as linen fragments in Egyptian tombs
Locked past touch in glass museum wombs

Were my thoughts to be spoken with ancient breath
Their layered pattern soon would dissolve in death
The loosening of their threads would rasp along the hall
Where cool museum cases float in still eonic pall

More intricate my suffering more silent too
Waiting centuries for interested gaze by you.

1986 #27

These Weeks of Rain

These weeks of rain are
minor in   The sad scheme of things
            Which were my standing tears to flow
      Would cover the chasmed globe.

1986 #27C

Distances

I see before me reaching out a great and open plain
With no disdain to mar its velvet honeyed cover offering
Lark ways undisturbed by sphynxes only wheat
As sand unending beckons birds and unheard gusts of air
For wideness does prevail
Beyond the chant of wings whirred there.

1987 #18

Nineteen Forty Four

We could not wake one morning
Our nightmare had no bounds

Our hell was all around us
The trumpet never sounds

They marched us out one morning
Bony cages incomplete
They plucked the cooties from our hair
They led us down a street

The street they led us down
Was packed with blood-tinged dirt
Its tracks were scratched by human nails
Nerves dead they could not hurt

They bathed us with warm waters
Our matted crusts did fade
We were wan and ghostly bathers
In a desolate charade

A few eyes were left to dimly
Perceive the strange new friend
Most eyes were fixed and blinded
By the horrors with no end

We gathered in a circle
Slowly dancing wretched figures
Objects of pity and sorrow
Caused by concentration camp rigors

The releasing soldiers stood
Amazed and shocked upon their ground
For them it was their morning
Our hell was all around

They washed the moldy misery
From off our crackled skin

But no rivers and no seas
Could stay the misery within

Pathetically we wreathed
Our new washed bodies on their arms
As mist and smoke we clung
In listless thanks they did no harm

Our cousins and our fathers
Piled as waste in moldering heaps
Our Jewish fate is not forgot
In memory it creeps

It echoes and it crawls
And it mourns and screams aloud
And it always lingers with us
Alone or in a crowd

It was a blessed morning when
The armies set us loose
Then we had no strength to judge it
As a blessing or a rouse

The reason that our god forgot
To hold us in his palm
And shield us from this horror
Lies a mystery in each psalm

We chanted in our centuries
We walked into our shuls
We walked as lambs and seldom lions
We rarely challenged rules

No matter and no reason
No good our souls to hound

We could not see the morning
For our nightmare was not bound

It reeked into our nostrils
It wrenched apart our soul
So our families and our people
Could nevermore be whole

They washed the skins and clothed them
They fed the mouths once more
They took us to new nations
To heal the fervent sore

We went along and woke up
We started in new jobs
We made new homes and schooled ourselves
In spite of inner sobs

But still we often wake now
With a nightmare feeling there
It will never wash away for good
It is always everywhere

We could not wake one morning
Our nightmare had no bounds
Our hell was all around us
The trumpet never sounds.

1987 #32

The Living Bird

I miss the lost art of lonely bird-watching
Replaced as it is now
By all those groups of well
Organized folk equipped with

Latest models of neat hanging binoculars
Assorted books to guide their eyes
And tape recorded bird songs done
For them by experts to conduct
The sounds they should perceive

I suffer greatly from the
Loss of solitude and from the
Loss of chance to fumble in
My way, to wander into woods
And hear a rustling and then
Feel my hopes arise as to the
Creature that might nest
There unaware and then to
Miss him catching only distant
Whirrs from corners of my eyes

While inward vision smiles
To form the spectacle within
Imagination sweet, a gorgeous yellow
Graceful bird less wide than long
From head to toe and sporting hats
Of pea green feathers mixed with
Purple threads and down his sides
A keen black stripe so clean it
Nearly cuts away the dazzling tail

Of orange specked with white
A most delightful bird
That undulates in flight
And hums Aida all day long
Until he tires of themes
To seek his slumber in some bush

I suffer greatly from the lost art of
Waiting for my bird in chill and dark
With no instrument to comfort me
Seeking to forestall the chance
Of missing him full view, my bird
Whose repertoire defies all
Nomenclature, yes whose whimsical
Adroitness might at any moment
Lead him once again to fly
In parabolic trance while
Whirling fast from side to side
If only to enhance his full
And happy feeling as he
Can't resist the soaring up
Of new tunes now
Of Turandot and later on
Some Wayfarer songs with disregard
For all the programmed bird tapes

A wicked warbler tricky and
Delightfully aloof, for even I
Who love this gleaming bird
And wait alone in woods
Of frequent damp with guideless eyes

Must once again create his image
If I hope to spot and watch
His brilliant yellow soars

In airy regions inhospitable to
Ornithology

I suffer greatly from the
Lost art of lonely bird-watching
Wishing I could shake the
Premonitions numbing me of
Vigil stands in stillness thick
While vast winds slowly glide by
Containing eons of spent dust
Of old mosquito wings suspended in
Salt spray mixed with particles of
Ancient Egyptian clay

I wait alone as if
Realizing that groups of those
Who watched bearing well equipped knapsacks
Of compasses and glass and maps
Are gone long since, their lists of birds
With greenish films of mold
Are strewn on forest floors
Those lists so old and accurate
I wait with imbecilic stare
For my bird to gleam and sing
In irresistible delight.

1986 #26

Old Celadon

That place has bowls of
Old celadon crackled and hushed

After years of sitting in
Chinese caves far away

Glass museum cases now
Embrace the bowls
No sound of gongs disturbs
Their surface nor
Can dust molest their
Climate controlled mouths

That place can telescope the decades
Distances between are dwarfed
By longer time the bowls endured
Across vast asian seas

There I can fix my gaze
Upon an old crackled vase
Of Chinese celadon then
Walk towards the courtyard
Ringed with plants
Around the still pool
To look upon the cold stones

       Until I force myself to curl
       Into a harder stone and colder
       But if pleased
       Some pale jade vase
       With deeply carved and
       Intertwining leaves
       Can hold my contentment well.

1988 #35

Coleus Plants

If the coleus plants, gorgeous in summer, and persistent in early fall, have
Finally given up their variegated wine and yellow and chartreuse colored
Leaves and stems, to droop sadly in their supporting earth, claiming that
Winter will be the real winner, then we do have to mourn somewhat for
The passing of these joy giving plants. If the busy squirrels that dashed
Relentlessly from tree to grass to acorn to tree, and madly stored away
Their winter supply of food, have now almost disappeared from view,
Preferring to hole up in their nests, then we are again forewarned of
Winter's intentions. If we look at grey skies whose only decorations
Are drizzle and broken twigs, then surely winter is coming along soon.
The defense for us is obvious. Store away lots of blueberry muffins, lots
Of chocolate truffles, jars of instant coffee, cans of chick peas, and
A few boxes of kasha and oatmeal and farina. Listen to baroque
Music when the darkness descends too early, and chorales can
Cheer. Beware of music played on so-called "authentic" instruments
Of the olden days, because we definitely do not want to be
Reminded of those empty days when there were no digitized
Recordings and we know for sure that Beethoven and Mozart
Would have gone bananas if they had the opportunity to compose
On the electronic magic that every kid can now use. The inventions
Took too long, and the musical geniuses became sparser and sparser.
It was really much better however, in the olden days, when their
Concept of war was just something to be fought between armored
Knights on hefty horses. Sadly many were speared, as great artists
Have since painted for us to remember, but no damage could be
Done long range with gruesome air mechanics and instant
Internet communications. So.... let there be baroque music
Played on our electronic digitized devices, but let us only have

Horses to ride, no tanks, and a few guys with shields and swords
To represent us in war. Which brings me back to the coleus
Plants which did finally give up their glorious colors in anticipation
Of ice and wind and empty tree branches and surrounding darkness.
We will hunker down now with our chocolates and chick peas and
Listen to the human voices of chorales.

21st Century MT

A Splendid Day

In the fullness of trees I rejoice at morning
In their rustling and one dark holly
Remaining still in shaded glossy splendor
As glorious rings of green
Surround my yard fully
And generously dance to the cool wind
Then rest in leafy stillness
Until the zither strikes again
To stir their leaves and brush the foliage
Skyward thus revealing paler green.

1987 #30

Grandchild

She sleeps sweetly on my desk
The photo of a baby blessed
With cuddly quilt her mother made
She naps in crib in peaceful shade
The pretty toys surround her head

Soft dolls and teddy-bears share her bed
And when she wakes, arms pick her up
To care for her and give her sup
She came into a cheerful house
Her room looks out on lettuce patch and roses bloom
Around about the doorway neat
They should for this granddaughter
Sugar plum sweet

1987 #27A

Events

At five weeks old she's innocent of Mozambique
Where other babes must stare benumbed
Where hunger is no surprise their
Only toys are pesky flies
That hover grimly round their faces gaunt
Round their tiny bellies swollen sick with want
Outdoors they remain for
Wander they must

Poetry, Essays & Other Original Works
Written by you

Last Flower of Summer

The song about the "last rose of summer" kept me humming in late June, when our weather had just become officially summer weather, very hot and very humid and unpredictable rain showers. I enjoyed going out into my garden and viewing all the flowers that were now in full bloom. Those orange and tall tiger lillies that had taken over almost two thirds of my garden and two thirds of all the neighboring gardens. Since I myself am not orange and certainly not tall, always being the shortest girl in class, these wondrous tall, orange flowers enchanted me. They were so different from me, and therefore I could look up to them, rather than having to crouch down low to view and weed some of the other summer flowers that were popping out. Like the bushes and bushes of chrysanthemums, from which one is supposed to snip off the early buds, to make way for the late comers. The late comers were early this hot and humid day, and so there were already a few white chrysanthemum flowers and a few pink chrysanthemum flowers interspersed down there.

I did miss the lilac blooms, long gone, and also the peony flowers, long gone, which required me to snip off the brownish remains, so next year new ones would bloom better. I had also spent several hours snipping off the dead azalea flowers from the several pretty blooming azalea bushes in my backyard. I had varied colored azalea bushes, that gave me a big and lasting palette of color for weeks in late Spring. There was one particular azalea bush however, that was planted all alone in a more distant and shady part of the yard, and it always was the last one to bloom, pink flowers. By now, all of this late blooming azalea bush was definitely finished blooming, and a week before I had trimmed its little branches at their tips to make room for the next year of retarded blooming azalea flowers. Of course, the iris flowers were all gone and the iris leaves turning brown also.

This hot and humid day at the start of official summer, had me going outdoors early in the morning, to then be able to stay indoors in mid-day where the air-conditioners and fans and cold drinks could help me survive the heat. With coffee cup in hand, I went out to my deck and gazed around, humming to myself about the "last rose of summer" which was how I was feeling. I sipped and gazed around, and sipped and gazed around until my gaze reached the shadiest part of the yard, overcast with the branches of evergreen trees. I suddenly dropped my coffee cup, in astonishment. It was an almost empty cup, do not worry. There, on that late blooming azalea bush, was a large beautifully formed pink flower. It was surrounded by dark green shadowy greenery, and stood out proudly.

Now I changed my tune. I happily saw the "last pink azalea of summer".

This late and extremely gorgeous bloomer gave hope to all of us. Never say die.

by Milicent G. Tycko June 25, 2013

FEB. 20, 2017 —1

This occurred to me in the afternoon, as I sat on my chair to catch some sun.

Jennifer the child was hugging Juniper, her younger sister, and their mother Joan looked on and gave a big smile.

She did this often while cooking for four. Her long time husband Jacob was outside hunting. He saved some meat, but mainly kept the sparkling teeth and antlers so later he could sell these to the other men in Johannesburg. The Jews

—2—

who like many had left their native land nearby and went to make their fortune in Johannesburg. Many were merchants, awaiting others who wanted a few antlers and teeth that sparkled like jewels. They made jewel rings to give to women who came from their native Jewish town. Many made towns. All needed huts and Jacob, who built that hut for four, was good at that. He had learned about building from his skilled father, named Jonas. Building the huts in new found wilderness was a long time generational skill. So Jacob adept returned for his meal and together the four ate and retired on mats on the floor. All night long, until sunshine did glow and Jennifer and Julep did hug and Joan did smile all the while.

And Nützl got up from her chair

This occured to me in the afternoon, as I sat on my chair to catch some sun:

Jennifer the child was hugging Junip, her younger sister, and their mother Joan looked on and gave a big smile

She did this often while cooking for four. Her long time husband Jacob was outside hunting, He saved some meat, but mainly kept the sparkling teeth and antlers so later he could sell these to the other men in Johannesburg. The Jews

who like many had left
their native land nearby
and went to make their
fortune in Johannesburg.
Many were merchants,
awaiting others who wanted
a few antlers and teeth
that sparkled like jewels.
They made jewel rings
to give to women who
came from their native
Jewish town. Many made
towns. All needed huts
and Jacob who built that
hut for four, was
good at that. He had

learned about building from
his skilled father named
Jonas. Building the huts
in new found wilderness
was a long time generational
skill. So Jacob adept
returned for his meal
and together the four
ate and retired on mats
on the floor. All night
long, until sunshine
did glow and Jennifer
and Julep did hug and
Joan did smile
all the while.

And Nitzi got up from
her chair to write of
her images now.

Feb. 20, 2017

This occurred to me in the afternoon as I sat on my chair to catch some sun:

Jennifer the child was hugging Junip, her younger sister, and their mother Joan looked on and gave a big smile

She did this often while cooking for four. Her long time husband Jacob was outside hunting. He saved some meat, but mainly kept the sparkling teeth and antlers so later he could sell these to the other man in Johannesburg. The Jews who like many had left their native land nearby and went to make their fortune in Johannesburg. Many were merchants, awaiting others who wanted a few antlers and teeth that sparkled like jewels. They made jewel rings to give to women who came from their native Jewish town. Many made towns. All needed hats and Jacob, who built that hut for four, was good at that. He had learned about building from his skilled father, named Jonas. Building the huts in new found wilderness was a long time generational skill. So Jacob adept returned for his meal and together the four ate and retired on mats on the floor. All night long, until sunshine did glow, and Jennifer and Julep did hug and Joan did smile all the while.

And Mitzi got up from her chair ???.

Beneath the heat their earth is dust
No water left for tears to form
They cannot cry beneath their
Dry and cruel sky.

Enjoy your toys my sugar plum
For now that is your part
But as you grow let pity and compassion swell your heart
Perhaps once you are grown and then
The world becomes your job
You'll care to find a way to quell
The sorrows and the sob

Then seeing far beyond your
Present rose-bowered life
You'll enter broad humanity
As poet, doctor, wife

You've made me a grandmother happy
With your myriad infant charms
Enabling me to hold again
All children in my arms.

July 1987 #29B

Waiting

The quiet limpid dark lies pooled green
Beyond a quiver
Held taut by algae skin

Before the birth deep lonely bells
Sound tonelessly in echo of
The centuries of spent man

Egyptian stillness caught in shrouds
Hangs poised awash in mourner's tears

The rock condensing lost life
The mountain peaks in frost

Saw Grandma Daisys' Russian friend later

Dec. 28

Dear Mitzi, Dan & Jonathan,

Hope you are enjoying the spring like weather altho I'm sure it won't last long. Its been rather unusual, but the unexpected changes in weather usually bring on colds etc.

We wish all of you good health and happiness throughout this coming new year of 1983.

Nothing much of news I can write about so far we are holding our own. Regarding the music (Alein in Weg).

My neighbor who is a Russian woman, and can read, write and talk the Russian language, gave her interpretation of the words by Lermontoff. She recognized the music. I just sang the melody to several Russians here, and they all knew it as it is a famous and lonely song. Not exactly a folksong, but more of a poetic, romantic one. You asked Daddy if he would translate it to English, as you could also sing it in English. However he said there is time for that. Next time I go to the library. I will see if there has been a translation of this particular number, since there are some by Pushkin and other poets Lermontoff is one, according to the woman who tried to explain it to me. A real translator will make it rhyme etc.

A few stamps for Jonathan, if he is saving any. One came with a lovely card from Sylvia, wishing all of us a happy happy New Year. Best of health. Joy in everything. She says, so far all is well there, with her anyway. This is the season for cold, wet weather in her locality. She will try to come out in the springtime. Love to all you Tycko

Mother Dad & ???

From the Russian

(1)

I go out on the road alone.
And there is a fog
A little path covered with gravel is visible (shines)
The night is quiet
And the meadow is listening to God
And the stars talk to each other

(2)

And the skies seem splendid and beautiful
The earth is asleep in an azure cover
Why is it so difficult my longing
Do I feel sorrow for anything?

(3)

I don't expect anything of life
and I don't feel sorrow about the past
I'm searching for freedom and rest
I would like to forget myself and fall asleep

(4)

Not by the cold sleep of the grave
I wouldn't like to fall asleep that way
In my breast there should be quivering
The strength of life so that when I breathe
The breast would slightly rise

(5)

That all night and all day
My hearing should caress a sweet voice
That would sing about love
Over me forever green
A dark oak tree should bend and whisper

Bespeak the endless gloom
And sorrow of cessation

Before the birth a pause recalls
All peoples gone and persons' pain
The empty vials of anguish stored
In recesses where only octopi seek grace
The deep respectful bells resound and fade
All salamanders stop
While eagles stare immobile

A lifted wave of mighty weight
Curls somberly above the sand
And joins the stillness all around
Poised captured as in prayer
Then crashes downward heavily
A thunder roll pervades the beach
The jungle screams its myriad birds

And we too sing out loudly as
The birth proclaims again

The will to live
The worth of it.

May 1987 #28

Princes of Air

Vain and lonesome princes of air
Surveying skies from mesas bare
In lieu of hilled castles white
Ancient marbled halls with

Bird-filled night
With raiments gold and gurgling pools
Of scented water which flows and cools
In lieu of nightingales and hare
The wind now whistles on mesas bare
The stars that gleam and brighten skies
No longer suffice to widen eyes

Within the concrete lab they wait
The princes of air to calculate
How to place their complex design
For modern skies both sinister and benign
A web of missiles and anti-ones
To invade former provinces of glorious suns

Where lolling princes once released
Their pulsing birds to fly
Now scientists grim on mesas send
Their metal into sky.

1985 #17

How to Leave the Old World
(on leaving France in 1962)

In this castle of my soul,
How queer to call it that,
How else
Rain desolate without
In night remains
A dull green river

Winding back and forth
Shadows deep and figures gold
The sparkling touches of my world drawn in,
What it is I know not

To drift to drift
Venetian dark, the bridges
Slowly walked upon
The marbled floors
The vaulted domes
Within me walks myself
Within the halls the corridors
The mirrored walls
Italian red
Who to claim the sun
The lake the olive grey

That softens all the green of me
Within the moat
A whitened stone
So smoothed again
By hands no more
The delicate within the gloom
That yawns about the fortified
This is my soul this now become
My European amalgamum.

Without, within, it matters not
But that the green be fresh
The velvet old the somber sad
The radiant bold
I cannot leave this other world
Kaleidoscoped within my tears
Will it then drop away
To earth in only momentary

Clear, circulating whorls
Of tears, pointed color
Pear shaped tastes
All of them to drop away
In tears of parting
(Just as then) when all
Of life is lost embraces
Only now within my soul
It periscopes to visions deep

All reflections manifold
Lifted teased as tissue fine
From life without
To hold now firm
In this castle on this hill
Near these banks
And through these halls
All is mirrored all is kept
Gilt-edged ivory hanging high
Over chasms undefined
To hold it all the soul decides
To name these castles
Draw these moats
Describe the hollows
Fix the ghosts.

1962 #54

Yizkor

Most of us go on living
The dead lie inert
Like figures in the carpet

Which we dance upon
As a bridge between two cold lands
My soul is pained by dark
And somber thoughts
Loved ones not here to know
The glistening iron bathed in
Radiant sun
That holds the bustling
Traffic of life
Surging ahead renewing itself

My face turns up to
Glory in the moments left
To smile against the
Treachery of death and loss.

1993 #46

Elegy

The bee lost within a flower
Seems justified
So is the moon correct to
Sink away at day
But now that you have
Sunk into your grave
It is all wrong
I moan alone within

This Yon Kippur is too late
For you to starve and
Meditate upon wrongs
Your body gashed with ills

Lies under earth
And flesh that thrilled to life

No longer touches or is touched
If then a flower or a weed
Is nurtured by this earth
It will not ease the mournful
Crying of my soul

So long ago so long ago
Part of my youth is buried
Part slashed through
So cruelly by your death.

1993 #51A

Poem

Death came to my door once more
Shuffling along in soft old slippers
With dust on their soles and
Water stained on top
He asked only to be welcomed
In his faded robe with arms
Weakly waiting to hold me
And carry me with tenderness
As they had when strong
When I died into the world
From the oblivion of the womb
When he held me up and
Laughed and wrapped me in
The soft cloths and small cap
For winter, then I saw

The cold and hard winter
But did not realize I was
Held and warmed and fed
And took my joy of life for
Many years, again the door
Is opened to this old and
Steady creature, death, who
Wants to hold me near the
Faded robe and tread softly
Away to the eternal winter
If he comes this way, gently
I will climb into the weakened arms and
Gladly go away.

August 2000

To Dan

I want you between the
Sheets of my soul
Lying dolefully forever
But you fled like the seagull

Leaving a feather
Upon the rocky shore

I want you, while the feather
Skips and whirls along the pebbles
Lifted by the wind
As crashing waters roar

More seagulls gather in an
Answering din of sound

Then scatter overhead as the
Tide pushed waves roar near again
Grey and white they soar
Against the fog drenched sky
Never still
Never standing quiet on their shore

As my longing for you
Rises restlessly
Suspended never ready to be
Lying still and dolefully forever
Dearest love.

1996 #47

To Dan

Thanks for fixing my tile
With your mighty file
Your wit and strength persist
You are so hard to resist
We pulse through life all the while
As my heart you do beguile.

2002

To Dan in April

When we lay intertwined as in
Translucent white near the chilly window
Glass that faced upon a wall of bricks

It seemed that we were floating in
Flames from myriad candlesticks

Within that tiny room of books
We dared to try our nakedness of soul,
In trust and weeping smiles
We turned and wondered at our
Happenstance to meet across huge miles

Repeating and returning to each other
As two pearly shells that
Tossed and rolled in waves
Upon the shore a groove was carved
In sand until for you the role of father found
For me the role of mother

Interweaving came the years
Beneath our trees to shelter
Children's limbs and songs
Those many years as sands that
Trickle through an hourglass
Became uncountable and swept in
Yearglass forming dunes

Deep oceans washed and washed against the dunes
And now the years with care are measured

In retrospect it seems the flames
Of imaged candlesticks reached out
Encircling us in love then
The chilly window glass seems vital still
That looked upon a wall of bricks
Translucent white we carved a life
As pearly shells carved paths
For waves to wash ashore

Incessantly when we by happenstance
Did meet across huge miles
With weeping smiles.

April 2002 #50

Bad Mood

If one is feeling downtrodden
The amusement presents itself
Of finding apt analogies
Is it like scaling a steep rocky
Wall with tired fingers or
Like slogging through cold wet
Mud with weakening legs or
Each day watching as the distant
Fog thickens and encroaches or
None of these cliches
Is it more like singing a song
And continuing to sing because
The emptiness of ceasing is
Uninteresting?

January 2002 #52

White Mountain Medley

In Spring the full snow-melted Pemigawasset River comes "brawling" down the White Mountains of New Hampshire to roar into the Merrimack River at Concord, then rush out to the Atlantic Ocean. But in late August the placid Pemigawasset River is pretty as it shows its multi-colored bedrock all through the mountains, like a variegated necklace of revealed jewels. In Winter the burdened Pemigawasset River fills again with heavy ice and snow, still carving away it's notches in stone, with only the hungry foot-prints of black bear, moose, fox, raccoon and others to decorate its gleaming surface.

Need I define a notch, which on a branch is only a small cut, and on a tree trunk may be a man-induced triangle of space still sore from the ax which cut it, and may fell a tree, and on a belt may be the miniscule change when tightened a bit by the increasingly malnourished wearer determined to be frugal, but on an ageless mountain is only river of ice made over long, silent time. The Pemi-Pemi-Pemi takes its time and always has. We give it a name, this wondrous sculptor of congealed dew and rushing movement. We call it a "river" and define its place, knowing it merges to all seas over all time. It nourishes bears and eagles and fish and feeds our desire for reliable beauty. We will visit again. Someday soon. Remain there.

August 1999

Norse

Norse, norwalk, normal, nice
Norse was neither worse
Nor cased in ice
Norwalk lies on maps all cut
Connected by the lines of red
Numbered highways numerous
Nicer though is Norse
Steeply mountained
Go there soon
Before the ice, when
Only drear piles of leaves fall

Along the rising tracks so
One train can lift you to the
Top of Norse and swiftly down to
The sea of Norse
Normal for the fish-eyed
Folk of Bergen
Humped against the wave-dragged wind
Normal in a Hanseatic
City poised for ice.

1998 #55A

In March

A pastel film guards the scene of
Brown and tangled limbs of trees

Restraining urgent buds
A pale grey sky allows now only
Blackbirds through the vacant
Interstices

With decency all noisy colors
Stand aside allowing thus
The soothing wash obscure protect
Withhold the crash of Spring
One day more before
Torrents of bright new green are seen.

1998 #55B

Winter

Winter winter I'm forlorn
I thought you went but you're not gone

My crocuses are shiver-ing
You fooled them into thinking Spring

Likewise my primroses do droop
Why don't you just jump through a hoop?

The world has turned but you pretend
That winter chill must never end

It's daylight savings time, you fool
So get ye hence, and that's a rule!

April 2001 #56A

The Fish in the Dish

A fish in scaley armor
Lay gasping on the plate
It wriggled and fluttered its gills
As it muttered "I think I prefer to not wait"

"The cook has returned with potatoes
From her numerous shopping trips
And that gleam in her eyes
Makes it hardly a surprise
She's preparing to cook fish-and-chips!"

With a heave and a sigh
To a cry of "oh my"
That fish leaped to the nearby sink
"By using my brain I will
Swim down this drain
To the ocean so blue, I do think."

"If they catch me once more
I'll lie on ice in the store
And wait to be chopped for a dish
I hear it will soon be Pesach so I
Can at last become tasty sweet gefillte fish."

So down through the sink
Went the fish who could think
And because of his courage and pluck
He escaped to the sea
And forever was free
What fantastic and marvelous luck!

April 2001 #56B

March 1999

Tamar, the gypsy girl (Serena, the gypsy girl)
Her damp black ringlets curl
Above her soft grey eyes

(Those eyes which hold the
Whole world's tenderness
Within their glance)

Tamar, the gypsy girl (Serena, the gypsy girl)
Is born to dance
In whirling glee

Above all else her gentle being
Is loved, it's no surprise
Her eyes contain the depths of lakes
The vastness of skies
And being a blessed girl
She will dance and fling
To all around, much happiness

#57

Dewey

Since I came home there are questions galore,
So I'll have to explain to prevent any more,
"Oh where have you been, little kitty of mine"
And "Tell us what happened in meows so fine".

Well, I kept hearing stories about a cat and his hat
It was getting quite boring to just lie on my mat
And over and over see pictures and movies
All featuring this hat, it all seemed so groovy.

I said to myself, "Maybe my hat got lost
That I used to once wear
I am bold, I will find it
I promise, I swear!

I snuck out the door when nobody was looking
They were all very busy with pasta a-cooking

And ran behind bushes and climbed up the trees
I hung from my tail like the circus chimpanzees

All the while I was seeking my own tall hat
Now tell me little children
What do you think of that?

I got so tired I had to rest
With one foot in the sparrow's nest
The other foot I used to scratch my head
The cicadas were bouncing all over my bed.

I looked in the mailbox and under the steps
I asked the doggies where it might be kept
But alas and alack no hat could be found
I was getting so dizzy from spinning around

My throat was dry and I needed a drink
"It's time to go home" I started to think
"Meow and meow and meow some more"
And finally, guess what, they opened the door.

Drink up little kitty, you don't need a hat
We love you without it, and here is a pat
Right on the top of your soft furry head
And now, all good children, it is time for bed.

By Grandma Mitzi
For Dewey and Ari and Serena

June 2004

Happy Father's Day at last to Dan,
The guy who said, "I think I can"
And like the little engine proverbial,
Without even taking anything herbial,
Not even an extra Vitamin C,
Said to himself, "This is really for me"
And thus his life for decades did commit
To caring for offspring, thinking "This is it!"

And thus by being quickly de-ci-sive
His time and salary he unstintingly did give
For honor, for glory, for country without pay
To rightly claim his place in two centurys' Father's Day.

He straddled the twentieth changing diapers buying bikes
Nose to grindstone even if there were tuition hikes
Into the twenty-first with eyes a-sparkling, glowing still
Surviving fatherhood, avoiding perils of gin-mill

So on this day for Fathers, we all only have just one,
Three times he justifiedly declares, "You are my son."
And slowly and with trembling bends three times to pat each head,
As in a Yiddish accent says, "I think I am so gled".

(This was written today by the girl he crowned with Motherhood)

Apologies to The Little Engine Who Could

Water Play

This is best performed within the reader's imagination. A play to read. The setting is a dining-room with wan greenish light streaming through the window. Simply furnished. A table and two chairs. Wallpaper faded as in a Vuillard painting. A man sits reading a newspaper in one chair. Across from him sits a woman. She jumps up from her chair.

Woman: Within the heart of thick cold waves dwell whitened fish and other pulsing life albinoed by the lightless prison in which they passively float. The ponderous waters bent by the moon contain these delicate creatures which anonymously cling to life much as fruitless hope flourishes midst doomed despair. The slamming tonnage of furious ocean in stormy mood, while railing sternly to disassemble sturdy ships, suffices not to crush this tiny life that easily would fill a hand with thousands were it scooped up from the deep. Nutrient microcosm in foamy folds of sea.

She remains standing quietly after speaking. The man reads his newspaper without looking up.

Woman: (speaking more softly now) Fastidious creatures persist in their evolutionary dances within the surging sea, wearing colorless delicacy modestly. They cannot care if they are seen, and can not complain if occasion traps them in a trailing net's coarse fibers, or even if a deep sea diver's bubble glass peers down their cartilaginous spines. (speaking in crescendo now) Numerically they win and man's intelligence in mighty brain struggles to manipulate centuries old accoutrements of verbal symbols merely to register and accentuate the wave's hidden life.
In despair the outnumbered human mind can lick its wounds by contemplating all the variegated filmy protoplasm that fills the former habitat of man.

The mind grasps solace, a singularly human mood, also in the creatures of the sky and earth that compensate for gloom. Our dusky moths and patterned butterflies and all the tiger-lillies of the fields and our humid canopies of green. We hold the figurative cool fishes in our hand with carelessness while listening intently for our birds.

She glances disinterestedly at the man who turns the page of his newspaper without looking up.

Woman: (speaking evenly) We recognize these songs as we can sing. Each of our dawns we wake to sympathize with feathered chatter, for we know they cannot stop, much as we must speak in endless circles with incessant murmurs, whether loudly to each other as on stage, or mumbling in poetic pathos quietly within ourselves. We churn as does the ocean, for the syballant sea has left a few eyedroppers full of salty fluid remembrances in interstices locked inside our greying brains. Pain it is to feel and it is pain to recollect and we are very well imprisoned in this swollen sea-gorged rhythm, just as the whitened organisms dwelling colorless in waves.

She sits down again.

Woman: (speaking in tidal beat) My father called me darling as he bore his aging cage of bones encasing cancerous glands. Others heard their mothers lisp upon them tenderly with lips that rounded out in screams of pain or froze in hopeless grimaces behind the screen. So my brain now reels in gloom when forced to recollect love's losses and urged to penetrate the hypothetical sphere defined by future loss and pain. The riptide twirls and churns the rocks at beaches' edges even as it does my thoughts, and makes of all soft strands of sand.

The man then looks up from his newspaper.

Man: (speaking nervously) Albeit magically the water remains hot within my cup, devoid of fish-like thoughts and momentarily craving only ground-up beans of humid green-canopied climes.

Woman: (speaking listlessly) Here's the instant coffee.

She is listening oft for birds.

END

1987 #31

Empty Shells

Shells spread upon the paper
Shiny pointy fluted speckled shells

Calcified carcasses lying still
Emptied of their crawling pulsing
Hungry sluggish sly and sticky life

These shells are beautiful quiet remote clean
A memory of what they had contained
Echoed and whirled within them once
Now their glossy sand-cleared chambers
No longer disturbed by this memory
Are able to gleam in constant silence
Exhibiting only their elegant stiff striations.

1991 #44

Age

Watery paste seems to glide over
All our moments
Sealing them in a
Distorted skin

A jar of thick glass
Stands mute on my desk
Reflecting light and
Drawing light in so that
Vivid white splashes are set off by
Silvery grey and
Black icey squares

So the years are coated in a film
Wherein pleasure glows through
Dim and darkened squares of time
And age serves to still the supple limbs
Until they seem as brittle glass

But no less glowing
No less lit.

1991 #45

At Montauk Harbor

It was a salty day of Indian summer. The water was glassy. It held the
fishing boats on a slick of water-skin. Two swans slid on the surface

between the boats. Swans approaching the shore. The lone seagull flying low met his reflection on the clear water. A single cormorant stood sentinel on a nearby post at the end of the fishing pier.

The eye was soothed. Thirty some fishing boats and sailing boats lingered quietly in their still moorings. A subtle crinkling of the water was the only response to the listless unquestioning breeze. A few tiny red and white striped flags hung above some of the boats in the harbor inlet.

The two swans skidded along the gray, white and blue brushstrokes which served as reflections of the boats on this lake-like crenalation of the outer sea. The swans were observed by the two older people who were themselves floated together in time. A flutter of his newspaper. A gentle sigh of her shoulders.

A moon of quiet joy seemed to bind them together.

As were the swans, as were the cormorant and seagull, as was the hushed and glassy lake with the outer sea.

1991 #43

Perimeters

A perimeter exists along the parrot's wing
Up around the part that does attempt to sing
The throat that gabbles crumbs to caw
A sound remote, no matter for I saw
The line continue round the feathered form
Encasing all its puffy green and bright markings

Exactly, and I felt perimeters attempt to be
Upon the edge of all the sea
But breathless lines could not regain stability
The foam at beach's shore
Though light and bubbly where it crept
Destroyed with ease and to the core
My concept of perimeters
It flowed in daring dashes toward the beach

Seeking once again to draw perimeters
My eyes alight on moist pebbles
Trod upon by sea-wrens, gulls and mussel-heaps
All choked by weeds from sea
There stay the smoothened rocks
Certainly a line defines each stone
For one appears a tan and white
Elongated egg
Seen in border, circumspect
Apart and hard, as you and I
Forget the sea, its surging and
Its openness

We took a break
In Greenport at the little store
Along the harbor side
There was a large straw basket
Filled with puffin toys of fake fur
Black and white with thickened beaks
Set upon the floor

Then we two stepped out
Escaping soap and candle smells
Into the sea-cleared air
Where a seagull stood upon
The planks of wood there

Its stiffened wings
Hardly ruffled in the spray
Until it soared away
Blending with the distant grey

Destroying thus perimeters
Its soaring flight akin to
Roaring motion of the sea
Whose salty fingers permeate the wings
In contrast to the
Fake fur bird basketed within

The noisy sea condenses me
The rushing waves in series seem to
Slap my mind with thoughts disjointed as
The floating planks of wood
Sent along the frothy edge of ocean's pulse

Recalling all those Mama's boys
Floating in their packed ships
To foreign soil
Toward battles defined by gunny turmoil
Tumbling from their ships like
Pebbles tossed along the shore
By reckless waves
While overhead the seagull flies
And cries out clear
The bird's wings splattered with
Sea spray too
As are the ospreys and the planes

As separate stones some luckless boys
Lie on sand in radiance cold
Their demarcation clear and told
To us bemoaning loss of bird

Confused by slapping waves heard
Near the fake fur puffin toys.

1988 #36

The Pink Fan

She sat rigidly at her desk trying to compose a feasible letter. Impossible. She felt mute with throttled anguish. The wastebasket was getting overloaded with torn-up fragments of disjointed phrases written with a furious speed and destroyed with equal rapidity. Luckily the swaying trees outside her open window had finally ceased their wind-blown pleading dance. The stillness of the humid night seemed to be laying down a thick cover over the landscape. The fringe of some tropical hurricane further south had combed through the tree-tops and gone elsewhere to vent its fury. She only wished the storm within herself could move on naturally to a new locale.

The pile of torn up papers accumulated, probably as the piles of branches ripped off in the path of the disappearing hurricane. The darkening cover of moist air almost became soothing to her. It persisted like an uncomfortable guest that one got used to in spite of the irritation. The small pink electric fan on her bureau made a distracting rhythmic hum, something like hush-again-and-hear-it, hush-again-and-hear-it. That one pink blade that was bent slightly out of line for so long gave the hum its special limping quality.

Her restless summer sleep was so conditioned to this pattern during these hot stuffy weeks, that it seemed easy for her now. She only had to turn on the small pink fan for drowsiness to take over. She wondered what would happen to her when the cold weather set in. She would have to wean herself off the hum of the pink fan and start listening for rattling windowpanes, or for sleet hitting the roof, or for branches snapping under the weight of snow. Such chores would be a welcome change from sitting in the middle of an obstreperous swamp of hot weather that never budged for weeks.

It was with grim gratitude that she suddenly remembered that tomorrow would be the day for garbage to be picked up. That meant she could empty the wastebasket and toss away all the damaging reminders of her inner storm. In broad daylight it would all come into focus. It would equate with the regularized surface of routine, and become just another household reflex. Clear and clean, clear and clean. In a way this amused her. This equating of her emotional upheavals as alternately expressed on paper and discarded with the bright motions of cleaning and clearing that the household day would bring. The automatic and necessary acts of wheeling out the garbage cart down the old driveway where grass clumps and weeds lodged in the cracks. She could perform this as if in a well rehearsed ballet taking place in the midst of the visual clues of lumbering trucks and the symphonic strains of their screeching, coughing, banging, jarring approach down the street. A nifty finality to all the communications passing through the household on paper; lined pages, scribbled notes, business letters, phone messages, lists and plans, calendar pages with weeks gone and crossed out, all those chores done. The human buzz melded into debris.

It reminded her of those grey paper wasp nests abandoned under the porch roof and those clay dabs of stuff along the tree branches left by insects, those wads of overturned turf she found in the mornings on the backyard lawn, left by the mysterious activity of underground nocturnal animals. Mere things left over. Shards.

As the hurricane fringes had now passed far away, so too her fury was passing. The humid cover of black night was inhabited by August cicadas outside the open window. The little pink fan was still humming.

Hush-again-and-hear-it. Hush-againand-hear-it. She broke away from her rigid crouch over the writing pad on her desk. She carelessly dropped the pen and watched it roll a few inches along the desk top. Then she walked thickly towards her bed and plunked down on it.

She was grateful for hush-again-and-hear-it, hush-againand-hear-it, hush-again-and-hear-it. The little pink fan's lullabye.

1988 #37

What I Think Now

One had better take along a handkerchief to this review
Because it seems that morbid images were vastly more than few
Back in the days when words were tagged to cold old lost mood
And my oft depressive feelings gave me fodder on which to brood
I am thankful that my habit of writing this all down
Served to alleviate gloom and let me go and hop around town
It all shows to go you that whenever life gets rough
You can summarize in paragraphs and write it on your cuff
But it also shows to go you that in writing it at all
One hates to really lose it like Cinderella's shoe at the ball
My doggie is a Basset Hound full of mischief like a pup
You never know what piece of shoe or sock she will vomit up
After having fun destroying it and shaking it to bits
That seems to me like some of my poems which are the pits
But then again it is fun sometimes to sniff amongst the ruins
Like the archaeologists. I suppose it's only human.

3-22-93

Squiggles Later On

The weather was getting chilly and some acorns
Were falling from the oak trees. One dark night we
Heard strange shuffling and running sounds coming
From the attic. This continued for a few days until
We wondered what was up there disturbing the normal-

Quiet atmosphere up there. So we called up a man
Who does carpentry and painting for us, and he
Showed up with his helper one day. He opened up
The outside wood of an entrance to the attic while
His helper went up into the attic from indoors.

Guess what? When the helper held a long broom-
Stick into the attic, a very cute and energetic squirrel
Ran right along the stick. Then the man who opened
Up the outside wood also swept out some leaves and
Twigs that were matted together to make a nest.

The workers hid in the bushes and think they saw
Some squirrels run out of the outside opening. But
Maybe it was just birds flying out of a nest in the
Eaves. Anyhow.... something did happen, we know,
Because from then on we never heard anymore of the
Shuffling and running sounds from the upstairs attic.

Someone who knows all about squirrels in attics
Told us that they like to nibble and bite the electric
Wires up there, to keep their pretty teeth nice and short.
So then we called up the electrician men to check our
Attic wires. Sure enough there was a lot of damage to
The soft coverings of many wires, so the electrician
Men had a big job up there to take out the bad parts
And put in new good electric wires. We did not want
To have any fires from old damaged wires. Can you

Blame us for that? We still have a sample of a well-
Nibbled wire to show curious children. Also, the
Electrician men found a few acorns up there. That
Made us think that there really were squirrels hoarding
Food for their warm winter nest in our attic.

Well we did miss the squirrel family. But not for long.
One day we saw Mamma Squiggles perched on top
Of our roof and signaling with her tiny paws to the
Squirrel children, Bing, Bong, and Baby Doll. To tell
Them which trees to scurry up on and where they
Could store more acorns for Winter. One day I
Looked out my window and saw Squiggles scurrying
Up the big pine tree, looking very well fed and happy.
When I go to the window and open the curtains, if she
Happens to be in the area, she promptly scurries up
The nearest tree to say hello.

I have learned a few things. It is really not good to
Feed peanuts to squirrels right on your own porch.
Then they decide to come into your attic. It is better
To say hello to them when they live in the wild, on
The lawn, on the trees, running across your driveway.

I have to go now, because I think I will look out
The window and wait to see Squiggles again.

MT 11/24/06

Perseus Perceived

There she stood all grace and fair
Her porcelain skin too young for wear

Were sapphires softened in white wisped skies
They truly would portray her eyes

Subtly blue with hopeful charms
Would Perseus clasp her in his arms.

2004

Granddaughters Four

She jumped upon the trampoline
Unseen her spirit motivating
Captivating all who sensed
Her strength and grace
Her willingness to leap ahead
        Without a care of risk
Or barriers intuit
        Only height and speed
Delighted her as upward fast
She streaked and left
A trail of wishes within cousins
        Yearning lovingly to
Follow upward on their own
Unique and daring twirls although
        Some spins replete with pause
        Some wary of the risk intuit
        Some barriers denied while
        Some in shyness hesitate

All of them, my granddaughters
Are wished a riskless joy enduring
Overcoming barriers and relishing
The paths ensuing
        Who could ever see what lies ahead
        My years of seventy six do not equip

Though arms of love as limbs of tree
Remain outspread
Forever reaching
Granddaughters four
Whom I adore
Relentlessly.

Milicent Tycko
December 2004

L. to R. Grandson Joshua
Granddaughter Sonia
Mitzi (grandmother)
Dan (grandfather)

L to R Granddaughter Sonia
Friend Joe
Husband Dan
Grandson Joshua

Scotch and Scots

Twas actually the Scotch
That brought us together
That time since, to gambol
Oft in soft heather.

Dark clouds at times do gather
Ayr they form dark storms
Twil always be the Scots'
Turn delivering no harm.

Green swaths carved by sun
Surround us for ages
Original love continually Burns
Attested to by sages.

Twas truly Scotch and Scots
(Spelling notwithstanding Loud drum rolls each commanding)
Tied years fifty-three with
Such strong knots.

July, 2005

Abated

As the swirling swooshing seas
Their shiny skins contract
Our fevers rage diminishes
And quivering less does act

Abated, quelled, reverberated
Waiting for the waves to slap again
The ship with louder tone
Our fevers race incessantly
Toward the final marble stone.

April 2005

Scottish War Memorial

I remembered that they died
(Jean-clad tourists milling round)
So I sat me down and
High above the stone-walked town
Cried

Carved above the entrance gate
Grey memories of that war called Great
(Is forties' war a footnote mere?)
Upon our hearts sore pain is
Seered.

Another footnote might be honed
To heavy incarved war called Great
We peer but find no final date
To carve yet deep in
Stone.

August 2005
Edinburgh Castle Memorial Hall

Oxford And Greenwich

From Bodleian to Butler
Progresses straight the path
To illuminated learning
Both of history and math

The stars above a mystery
Whose paths all seemed to vanish
Until with bright alacrity
You parsed the text in Spanish.

August, 2005

Cuisine

Pas d'asperges
Pas des courgett-e
Gateau seulement
Pour gentile Sonieta

August, 2005

Crickets

Once upon a cricket seen
A sliver slight of apple green
While waving wound about its form

Waft wisps of grass as silk from corn
The sliver stirred and shadowed green
Beneath the silk an eye was seen
To move in blinking hop within
The net of strands towards cricket kin
Amalgamated now with greenish others
Maybe sisters, maybe brothers
Once upon the crickets seen
Rejoicing all in brighter green.

June 29, 2006

From the Hospital Bed

Outside the Window

Belly-dancing Bobolinks
Bemused me
Darting and rolling from
Tree to tree
Incessantly.

July 20, 2006

The Inside Curtain

Elongated feathers
Of lightest blue
Float ubiquitously
On their lattice work
Geometrized

July 21, 2006

Inside Me

A poem buried in rubble
Obscure
Surely is deeper and
Sillier or
Conveying dim
Paths of
Long lost stars

July 21, 2006

Outside the Window Again

Oi oi oi mama mia
Only if and ans were pots and pans
Or hardware stores were gone
                With drifting sands
Oi only if this window scene of
Grayish blue water holding up
The island there,

Holding up the blurry land
Surrounding all with silvering grey
Waters galore up to the shore
Oi again oi vey is me
If only it could really be a
Place to stroll along
Sing Osloian songs
And not the window scene

Of shore
From hospital bed
Unchanging.

July 23, 2006

Imperatives

Write or be vanquished!
Now cease or be anguished,
Always.

July 23, 2006

Retrospective

Asides are always unawesome
Comments are uncrucial
Poems persist persevering
Sprung solely unsequential
Revealing only lightstriving
Saving from captured body
Pain stabbed body
Wrapped in days hopeless
Hospitalized eternalseeming
Comments are uncrucial
Words are wispy ladders
Promising escapes falsely.
Retrospective memories

Captured wisps from
Captured body.

October 1, 2006

And that's all she wrote—
well — for a while

Milicent G. Tycko
3/1/08

This occured to me in the after noon, as I sat on my chair to catch some sun:

Jennifer the child was hugging Juniper, her younger sister, and their mother Joan looked on and gave a
big smile

She did this often while cooking for four. Her long time husband Jacob was outside hunting. He saved some meat, but mainly kept the sparkling teeth and
Antlers so later he could sell these to the other men in Johannesburg. The Jews

who like many had left
their native land nearby
and went to make their
fortune in Johannesburg.
Many were merchants,
awaiting others who wanted
a few antlers and teeth
that sparkled like jewels,
They made jewel rings
to give to women who
came from their native
Jewish town. Many made
towns. All needed huts
and Jacob who built that
hut for Fours, was
good at that. He had

learned about building from
his skilled father named
Jonas. Building the huts
in new found wilderness
was a long time generational
skill. So Jacob adept
returned for his meal
and together the four
ate and retired on mats
on the floor. All night
long, until sunshine
did glow and Jennifer
and Julep did hug and
Joan did smile
all the while.

And Mitzi got up from
her chair to write up
her images now.

Feb. 20, 2017

This occurred to me in the afternoon, as I sat on my chair to catch some sun:

Jennifer the child was hugging Junip, her younger sister, and their mother Joan looked on and gave a big smile.

She did this often while cooking for four. Her long time husband Jacob was outside hunting. He saved some meat, but mainly kept the sparkling teeth and antlers so later he could sell these to the other man in Johannesburg. The Jews who like many had left their native land nearby and went to make their fortune in Johannesburg. Many were merchants, awaiting others who wanted a few antlers and teeth that sparkled like jewels. They made jewel rings to give to women who came from their native Jewish town. Many made towns. All needed hats and Jacob, who built that hut for four, was good at that. He had learned about building from his skilled father, named Jonas. Building the huts in new found wilderness was a long time generational skill. So Jacob adept returned for his meal and together the four ate and retired on mats on the floor. All night long, until sunshine did glow, and Jennifer and Julep did hug and Joan did smile all the while.

And Mitzi got up from her chair to write up her images now.

Printed in the United States
By Bookmasters